Welcome to ALADD[IN]

If you are looking for fast, fun-to-read stories with colorful characters, lots of kid-friendly humor, easy-to-follow action, entertaining story lines, and lively illustrations, then **ALADDIN QUIX** is for you!

But wait, there's more!

If you're also looking for stories with tables of contents; word lists; about-the-book questions; 64, 80, or 96 pages; short chapters; short paragraphs; and large fonts, then **ALADDIN QUIX** is *definitely* for you!

ALADDIN QUIX: The next step between ready to reads and longer, more challenging chapter books, for readers five to eight years old.

Read more ALADDIN QUIX books!

By Stephanie Calmenson

Our Principal Is a Frog!

Our Principal Is a Wolf!

Our Principal's in His Underwear!

Our Principal Breaks a Spell!

Our Principal's Wacky Wishes!

Our Principal Is a Spider!

Our Principal Is a Scaredy-Cat!

Our Principal Is a Noodlehead!

The Adventures of Allie and Amy
By Stephanie Calmenson and Joanna Cole

Book 1: *The Best Friend Plan*

Book 2: *Rockin' Rockets*

Book 3: *Stars of the Show*

Book 4: *Costume Parade*

Harvey Hammer
By Davy Ocean

Book 1: *New Shark in Town*

Book 2: *Class Pest*

HARVEY HAMMER

S.O.S. Mess!

BY
Davy Ocean

ILLUSTRATED
BY
Aaron Blecha

ALADDIN QUIX

New York London Toronto Sydney New Delhi

With special thanks to Paul Ebbs

ALADDIN QUIX
Simon & Schuster Children's Publishing Division
1230 Avenue of the Americas, New York, New York 10020
First Aladdin QUIX paperback edition February 2024
Text copyright © 2024 by Working Partners Limited
Illustrations copyright © 2024 by Aaron Blecha
S.O.S. Mess! is a Working Partners book.
Also available in an Aladdin QUIX hardcover edition.

Simon & Schuster: Celebrating 100 Years of Publishing in 2024
For information about special discounts for bulk purchases, please contact
Simon & Schuster Special Sales at 1-866-506-1949 or business@simonandschuster.com.
The Simon & Schuster Speakers Bureau can bring authors to your live event.
For more information or to book an event contact the Simon & Schuster Speakers
Bureau at 1-866-248-3049 or visit our website at www.simonspeakers.com.
Designed by Karin Paprocki
The illustrations for this book were rendered digitally.
The text of this book was set in Archer Medium.
Manufactured in the United States of America 1223 OFF
2 4 6 8 10 9 7 5 3 1
Library of Congress Control Number 2023947483
ISBN 9781534455191 (hc)
ISBN 9781534455184 (pbk)
ISBN 9781534455207 (ebook)

Cast of Characters

Harvey Hammer: Young hammerhead shark

Hettie: Harvey's older sister

Mom Hammer, aka Hanna: Chief of police; mother of Hettie, Harvey, and Finn

Dad Hammer: Father of Hettie, Harvey, and Finn

Spike: Puffer fish classmate and Harvey's enemy

Mr. Halo: Seafari tour guide

Flash: Turtle classmate and Harvey's best friend

Poppy: Hettie's best friend

Jason Jett: Number one racing clam driver

Finn: Harvey's baby brother

Craig: Mr. Halo's assistant

Principal T. Una: School principal

Rocky: Barnacle classmate and Spike's best friend

Contents

1

Seafari!

WOOOOOOOOOOOOOM!!!

SMAAAAAAAAACK!!!

CRAAAAAAAAAASH!!!!

DOINNNGNNNNGGG!!!

Okay, I can see that this might take a little bit of an explanation.

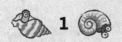

I'm **Harvey Hammer,** a hammerhead shark, and I'm trying to ...

1. Think up the next **installment** of my King Krusher and Hammer-Boy comic, where Hammer-Boy chases evil Cruz the Catfish Burglar....

2. Dodge the mountain of books on the kitchen floor and not get crushed by them....

"HAAAARVEY!" That was my older sister, **Hettie.**

She's always shouting at me. (She would say "raising her voice.") But I could tell she was *really* angry because she had her fins folded over her chest.

"That's my term paper **research** you've knocked all over the place!" she screeched.

"I'm sorry! I didn't expect a whole library right in my path. I'll clean it up," I said.

Well, I *tried* to say that, but . . . **DOINNNNNNNGGGG** . . . my hammerhead got stuck between

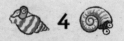 4

the oven and the refrigerator, so it was hard to talk.

"Oh, Harvey! You're *always* into into something. Let me help," Hettie said.

She grabbed my tail and tried to pull me out, but my hammerhead flubbered like crazy.

Why couldn't I have a sleek tiger-shark head? Not one that looked like it escaped from a toolbox! It was always in my way.

Finally, with one last tug from Hettie, I popped out.

 5

Once I was free and things had settled down, I held up one of the fallen books.

The cover had a picture of a little leggy air-breather who looked like he was jumping up and down on some strange device.

THE SCIENTIST'S GUIDE TO
LEGGY AIR-BREATHERS
(LABS)
(THAT'S YOU HUMAN BEINGS. NOT SHARKS.)

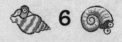

"So weird," I said.

Hettie answered, "It's not *weird*. It's *science*. I bet they probably think *we* are weird."

I guess she was right. I asked her, "Isn't doing *science* homework during vacation the most weird of all?"

"Harvey, you'd lose your hammer-head if it weren't attached to your body. **Mom** and **Dad** are taking us all to Seafari Park to see real humans in their natural **habitat**, remember?"

Oh wow! Hettie was right, I

had forgotten. And I soooooooooo wanted to go to Seafari Park to see those LABs.

Visitors to the park can see people throwing pebbles into the ocean, lying on towels, and getting angry when they get sand in their snacks and sandwiches.

I mean, the LABs even call them *sand*wiches—why would anyone get annoyed when there is actual sand in them? So weird!

Spike, a puffed-up puffer fish

from my class—who isn't exactly my best friend—went there last **semester**. He bragged how he got so close to a LAB, he poked it with one of his spines and made it run away. Everyone at school treated him like he was a superhero.

But I'm the one who knows all about superheroes. I bet I could get just as close as Spike. Plus, if the humans saw me, they'd be way more scared of me.

I had to prove I was as brave as

Spike. As Hammer-Boy would say, *Mission on!*

That was going to be the best day ever. At least, that was my plan.

2

LABs

The day had finally arrived, and we were crammed into a small tour bus. Mom and Dad had let each of us bring a friend. I'd brought **Flash**, my best friend and the fastest turtle in Coral Cove. He's also the biggest

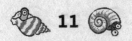

fan of my comics. He even has one of my homemade King Krusher stickers stuck on his racing clam helmet.

Our tour guide was **Mr. Halo**, an angelfish with bright white false teeth. "Up ahead, you'll see the gates of Coral Point Seafari Park!" he announced.

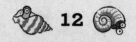

"I don't think I will be able to see *anything* if he keeps smiling," I whispered to Flash. "It's like he's got a bunch of glowing algae in his mouth."

"Excuse me? Mr. Halo?" Hettie was holding up her fin. "Is it true LABs like to gently bake themselves under the sun and then eat frozen food to cool themselves down?"

Poppy, a squiggly octopus, was Hettie's best friend. She was taking notes with a penfish and a notebook suckered to the end of her **tentacles**.

I groaned. When Hettie and Poppy were together, they were a total nightmare. When they weren't being know-it-alls, or bossing me around, they liked to practice this totally lame FishTok dance: the Seaweed.

What good is a silly dance anyway? It doesn't save people like a super-hero can. Big sisters, eeewwww.

"That is the theory," said Mr. Halo, answering Hettie's question.

He pointed to the distant shad-ows of humans, who seemed to be splashing around on the surface.

He continued, "Once we are on the larger bus, you will **observe** LABs behaving as they do: looking for strange food that looks like pink or blue fluffy clouds on a stick, or swatting a ball back and forth over a net, or burying themselves in the sand. **Very, very odd!**"

Mr. Halo slapped his fins together. "We are about to enter **amphibious** mode. Please remain in your seats and keep flippers, tentacles, and fins inside the bus."

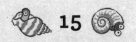

Just then Flash charged to the back of the bus to watch a Jet Ski zoom away, leaving a flurry of bubbles in its wake. "That's faster than **Jason Jett**, the number one racing clam driver in the seven seas!"

Hettie and Poppy were so happy, they started doing the Seaweed. I tried looking the other way as the excitement built in my tummy. We had gone from the small bus to this ginormous one.

It was made of five enormous lion's mane jellyfish, which were like separate carriages. Each was longer than a whale, and they swam so we could sit inside them. Their tentacles dragged behind us for what seemed like miles.

Slowly the bus moved out of the **shallows** onto a rocky patch of beach. Seawater filled up the jelly-fishes' bodies, so those of us with gills could breathe. Everyone had their noses and eyes pressed against the windows.

Sunlight burst through the water all around us. The beach, along with towels, beach chairs, sandcastles, and all sorts of weird and wonderful leggy air-breathers, came into view. I was just about to ask Dad for his binoculars. I was hoping I could spot a human to sneak up on, when . . .

"Okay, everyone. The tour is officially over," shouted Mr. Halo. "That's enough! It's time to head home!"

"What?" I screeched as the bus reversed away from the humans.

"We haven't seen anything yet!" Hettie added.

"Well, that's quite enough excitement for me," said Dad, who was **clutching** my baby brother, **Finn**, so tightly that it looked like Finn might throw up all over him.

Mom was barely paying attention since she was busy with her shell phone. She had a very important job, and sometimes she couldn't join in the fun.

"Did you see the way the people walked around?" said Dad. He was

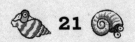 **21**

shivering. "Just walking like that, like a crab who's lost most of its legs. All but two. Just two walking legs. I don't like it at all."

"Hey, there's nothing wrong with having two legs," said **Craig**, Mr. Halo's assistant, popping his crab head out from his hermit shell with a giant grin.

Hettie stormed up the aisle toward Mr. Halo.

"But Poppy and I need to write down our observations," she cried. "We have a paper due."

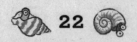

"I'm sorry," Mr. Halo replied. "If you read the small print on your tickets, you'll see there's nothing **guaranteed**. And if I feel you're in danger, I have to cut the trip short."

I sank **glumly** into my seat. If I didn't see any LABs up close, Spike would never let me live it down. And I'd never feel like a superhero.

Craig sat on the armrest next to me. "It's always the same. Nobody ever gets to see much anymore."

"Why?" I asked.

"Well," he began, "there was an

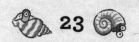

incident a few months ago, but—"
He stopped talking abruptly.

Mr. Halo pulled a screen down
from the ceiling. "We do have film
of leggy air-breathers. This one is
narrated by Dr. Jacques Crusteau."

Everyone applauded.

I quickly made my way over to
Flash. "We have to see a real person."
I tapped my fin against my Hammer-
Boy T-shirt. "Hammer-Boy . . . ready
for action. We have to prove to Spike
we are just as brave as he is."

Flash tapped his King Krusher

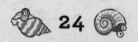 24

sticker. "King Krusher is ready for action."

We high-fived.

"Mission on!" we said.

No one was watching us as we sneak-swam toward the beach.

"We'd better not be too long," I said as I **thrashed** my tail and Flash paddled as hard as he could. We zoomed through the water along the shoreline. "But I need to do this, or I'll never be able to show my face at school."

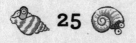 25

Luckily for us, there were some leggy air-breathers splashing by the shore and on the beach, doing that thing Mr. Halo had mentioned: smacking a ball back and forth over a net.

I raised my body to get a better look at them.

And that was when the screaming started.

"ARRRRRRRRRRGH!!! NO!!! GET OUT OF THE WATER!!!!

"THERE'S A SHARK IN THE WATER! IT'S COMING TO EAT US!!!"

Uh-oh!

What had I done?

3

Turtally Gone

PERSHWOOOSH!!!

I belly-splash-dove back below the surface, but I knew the damage was done. Leggy air-breathers don't like to see sharks' fins in the water where their floppy legs are paddling. Not that I was going to bite any of them!

Gross!

I looked around for Flash in the choppy waters.

Nothing.

Where was my best friend?

I tried to use my special Hammervision. It's a sixth sense that allows us hammerheads to send **signals** into the water to locate stuff.

It's the one thing I can do even better than Hettie.

PING! PING! PING!

I was sensing the humans up on the beach. Even as the waves calmed down, I could hear them. Some were shouting; others—their children, I

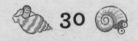

guess—were crying. But there was no sign of Flash at all.

I was pretty sure he hadn't gone behind me, back out to sea and the bus. So the only thing for me to do was go forward, toward the shore.

Keeping my head and fins down, I swam toward the seabed. It was rocky and lumpy with coral in thousands of colors and shapes. Flash could have been anywhere.

I turned my hammerhead left and right to get the widest spread of signals back to my Hammervision.

And then I heard:

"HARVEY!

"HELP!

"HELP ME!

"I'M BEING CHASED BY LABS!"

As I looked around, I could see what looked like a bunch of words hanging in the water. Two things struck me about them.

They were made from foam, churned out by a sea creature with their tail. (We call it trail-writing.)

I immediately knew it was FLASH'S trail-writing!!!

I recognized it because I had been the one who taught him how to rotate his tail, all whizzy and splashy, to create words in white, bubbly foam.

The words would hang in the

water for about thirty seconds. So that meant—I hoped—that Flash wasn't far away!

I hammered my way through Flash's trail-writing, smashing the words apart.

I sped over a rocky **outcrop**, past a coral garden, and then right up to the water's edge. I saw glittering rock pools. Some were tiny, some were huge, but they were all full of life. I flicked on my Hammervision, trying to see if I could spot Flash.

Yes! There he was! *But no!*

He was trying to escape from a little human who was chasing after him.

Flash seemed to be getting away. ***NOOOOOOOO!!!***

There was another kid straight ahead, holding a large bucket. This little LAB easily headed off Flash.

"Help me!!! Help!!!" Flash

screamed. They had caught him.

Suddenly something, or someone, tugged on my tail.

Oh no!

Was it a LAB?

"Would you watch where you're swimming?" a voice hissed.

I jumped up so high, I could have done a triple tail-end somersault before I splashed back down into the water again. But instead something stuck fast against my fin and held me in place.

"This is our spot, Harvey—find somewhere else to hide."

It was Hettie! Poppy was with her. It was her tentacle that had **suctioned** me.

"What are you doing here?" I whispered.

"Do you think you're the only one who can sneak off a tour bus?" Hettie answered.

Poppy chimed in, "We needed our observations!"

"Well, did you two observe Flash

getting turtle-napped by a couple of

tiny humans?"

"Of course we did," said Poppy,

waving a notepad and penfish in her

other tentacles. "Quite remarkable."

"Don't you think we should rescue him?" I cried.

Hettie looked annoyed. But then she sighed. "I guess so." She nodded at my T-shirt. "You're the superhero. What do you think we should do, little brother?"

Good question, I thought.

I lifted one eye out above the water. The little LABs were sitting by the water's edge, laughing and poking their fingers into the bucket.

"Harvey, can you hear me? Help!!"
Flash's voice sounded far away and
really scared.

I had to think of a plan, and fast.
There wasn't a second to lose to
save my best friend, who was either
going to become someone's pet—or
worse, turtle soup.

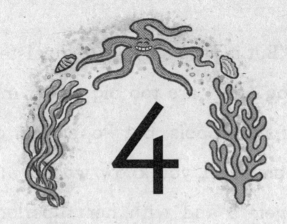

4

The Esc-Sea-Scape!

A superhero not only has to act fast, they also have to think fast.

I'd just finished outlining my plan. Unfortunately, Hettie was not buying it. "No way! You can't send Poppy over there. **It's too dangerous!**"

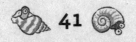

"But it's the only way," I insisted. "You and I are too big to get into the rock pools, but Poppy can do it, being all, you know, wobbly and boneless and with her superlong tentacles."

I stared at Poppy and then at Hettie. I swallowed. I wasn't going to enjoy this. I opened my mouth and tried to force the words out. *"Ple . . . le . . . le . . . eeeaa . . . shh . . ."*

Hettie frowned. "What was that?"

"P-P-Pl-Ple . . . PLEASE!!! You have to help. Flash needs us. And

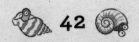 **42**

we have to hurry, not only for him, but before Mom and Dad and Mr. Halo discover we are all missing!"

Poppy tapped her beak with her penfish. "I suppose," she said, "the plan could work."

"Great, so you're in," I said, slapping Poppy on the back. "It's going to require split-second timing."

"But we are going to need a **distraction**," added Hettie. "We have to be super sneaky." Her eyes gleamed at me. I didn't like that look. Not at all.

Poppy slipped, slid, and crawled on her tentacles until she quietly dropped into the rock pool next to the bucket.

Luckily, the little humans were too fascinated with poking Flash to

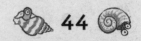

notice Poppy. I waited until she was close enough to reach up with her tentacles, then began my part of the plan. . . .

Hettie raised her fins.

"A-one, a-two, a-one, two, three, four!" she counted.

I began to ripple my fins and spin in the water, causing waves and bubbles to churn the surface.

"Keep in time with me. Come on, Harvey," said Hettie.

"I'm trying, but it's not working," I said.

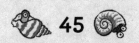 45

Then I started dancing.

And not just any dance.

I was doing *that* dance.

The goofy one from FishTok that Hettie and Poppy were **obsessed** with.

I was doing . . .

the Seaweed!

Urgh.

"Maybe now you should also try singing?" she suggested.

"Singing? You can't be serious?"

"I am," Hettie told me. "Poppy and I love making up songs to FishTok dances."

"*You* sing then," I said.

"You said you'd do anything to rescue Flash, didn't you?" Hettie reminded me.

She was right. I kept my flippers wiggling as I began to wail:

"I'm a hammerhead shark,
swimming in the sea.
With my big ol' head,
I'm easy to see."

"That's kind of good," said Hettie. "Keep going."

"I love to play,

all day and night.

But I won't eat you,

all right?"

One by one, the little LABs looked up from poking Flash as I sang and danced.

"It's working!" said Hettie as she moved along with me.

"I'm a friendly shark

with a funny head.

Fluhp-fluhp-fluhp-fluhp,

 49

let's all dance instead!

I won't hurt you,

I'm just here to say,

'Fluhp-fluhp-fluhp-fluhp,

let's have some fun today!'"

I shook my tail, flubbered my head with one fin, then the next, nose-shimmied to the left, side-swam to the right. I rose out of the water and waved my dorsal fin like I'd be shaking it all night.

Incredibly, the kids started to

move toward us one by one.

Hettie and I danced faster and faster, and as the kids moved far enough away from Flash, I sang at the top of my voice. . . .

"*Now, Poppy, now! Do it now!*

Pull it over fast, do it somehow!

I've got no more song left to sing.

I've even run out of rhymes;

we must go now.

See? Nothing rhymes at all!

Dooooooooooooo it!"

Poppy reached up, curled a tentacle around the bucket handle, and pulled.

It fell over, and Flash flew out on a gush of seawater.

"Harvey! I'm free!" Flash shouted.

The kids didn't know whether to look at me or Flash in the swirling waters. As they stood around,

confused, Flash and Poppy **scuttled** past them and into the open water.

I wanted to whoop, but before I could even open my mouth, I heard the kids spring into action. In the surf, their feet—which had rubbery-looking flat things attached—were making a *floop-floop-floop* noise as they splashed through the water.

They sure didn't look happy. They'd lost their turtle and looked determined to grab any one of us again. They started running our way.

Fortunately, in the ocean the four of us could move much faster than the little LABs.

"You three go ahead," I yelled at Hettie, Poppy, and Flash. "I'll make sure they don't catch us."

"Are you sure, Harvey?" Hettie asked.

"A superhero always takes care of his family and friends," I told her as I flipped and twirled, churning up the waters so we could all zoom away safely.

5

Flip-Flop Flip

"But what is it?" Flash asked.

"I have zero idea," I replied.

"Hide it, Harvey," Hettie whispered. "Mom and Dad will never take us on a trip again if they find out we snuck away."

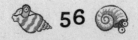

One of the little LAB's rubber shoe-y things had gotten stuck on my fin. Flash and I were both looking at it, totally confused.

We had all snuck back onto the tour bus just as the Dr. Jacques Crusteau film was ending. Luckily, no one had

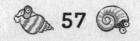

even noticed we were gone.

I started to put the floppy thing in my bag, but Hettie tapped me on the hammer. "Hey, do you think Poppy and I could get a closer look at that when we get home?"

"Er . . . sure," I answered, and handed it over for whatever silly reason Hettie wanted it.

The next day back at school, every class was in the auditorium. It was time for the presentations of the Coral Cove School science club.

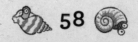

Principal T. Una swam up to the stage and introduced everyone and their projects.

We sat through three on bassball, two on how Kelp Krispies were made, and a couple of random ones about growing different flavors of seaweed and making hats from coral.

Then it was Hettie and Poppy's turn.

"To finish off the presentations," Principal T. Una began, "we have Hettie Hammer and Poppy Squiggle. It's about their latest research on the

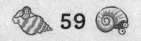 59

leggy air-breathers they saw on a trip to Seafari Park!"

"You know, everyone, I went to Seafari Park and managed to touch a LAB," said Spike loudly. "I poked it with my spines, and it ran away *terrified* of me. That's how brave I am."

Onstage, Hettie cleared her throat. "The LABs do everything differently from us." And then she and Poppy went on to tell everyone about the pink and blue food, goofy games, and how they sat under umbrellas even though it wasn't raining.

Suddenly Spike yelled out from the audience, **"This is boring!"**

"Yeah!" shouted his best friend, **Rocky**. "So boring!"

Hettie continued, **ignoring** them. "I've seen LABs cover their eyes with black glass when it's sunny, and they pretend to be fish. A *lot*. Swimming about and splashing."

Then Hettie took out the little human's rubber shoe, held it up, and announced, "This amazing leggy-air-breather object was discovered by our fellow researchers, Flash and Harvey."

Everyone gasped and turned to look at us. I felt a warm glow spreading in my tummy.

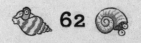

"It was *very* risky and dangerous," said Hettie, looking at me and Flash.

"And I almost got turtle-napped by some LABs, but Harvey, Hettie, and Poppy saved me by doing the Seaweed!" shouted Flash.

"Wow! That's amazing!" everyone cheered. "What an awesome idea!"

"That's nothing!" said Spike, puffing up to twice his size. "I bet they just found those things on the seabed."

Principal T. Una went back to the

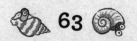

stage. "That's not nothing, Spike. I think we can all agree that this is a fascinating project that gives invaluable information. It deserves an A-plus. For *all* the researchers.

Harvey? Flash? Would you come up here, please?"

Huh? In a daze, we both swam onto the stage. "Wow," I said to Hettie. "This is the first A-plus I've ever gotten. Thanks!"

"It feels pretty super, doesn't it?" the principal asked, and winked.

It sure did. Suddenly Poppy, Flash, and Hettie started doing the Seaweed.

Everyone went wild!

And as I began dancing with

them, I bet that even King Krusher and Hammer-Boy couldn't have felt more like superheroes than I did at that minute.

Word List

amphibious (am•FIH•bee•us):
Made to be used both in the water
and on land

clutching (KLUH•ching): Holding
tightly

distraction (dih•STRACK•shun):
Something that makes one lose focus

glumly (GLUM•lee): Sadly

guaranteed (gare•un•TEED):
Promised to happen

habitat (HAH•buh•tat): Where a
plant or animal is normally found

ignoring (ig•NORE•ing): Not paying attention to something

installment (in•STAWL•munt): One part of an ongoing story

observe (ub•SURV): Watch or study closely

obsessed (ub•SEST): Overly interested in something or someone

outcrop (OWT•crahp): A large rock poking out from the ground

research (REE•surch): Careful study of a subject

scuttled (SKUH•tuld): Moved in a hurry

semester (suh•MEH•stur): One part of a school year

shallows (SHAH•lowz): Place where water isn't deep

signals (SIG•nuhls): Actions or movements used to warn someone or give information

suctioned (SUCK•shund): Pulled in toward something

tentacles (TEN•tih•kulls): Long, thin body parts used for feeling or taking hold of things

thrashed (THRASHT): Moved wildly

Questions

1. Why did Hettie and Poppy want to go to Seafari Park?

2. Who else in Harvey's class got to see leggy air-breathers up close?

3. Why didn't Harvey's father like the leggy air-breathers? What did you think scared him most about them?

4. What other names can you make up for human beings?

5. What piece of clothing got stuck on Harvey's fin?

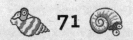 71

LOOKING FOR YOUR NEXT FAST, FUN READ?
BE SURE TO MAKE IT ALADDIN QUIX!